This book is dedicated to Joel Armstrong, the "Duck Man," who rescued the ducklings as they flipped and flopped, tumbled and plopped to Riverside Avenue in downtown Spokane. This book is also dedicated to my favorite duck of all time, Webby Duck Duck, who hatched in my classroom and gave my students and me loads of joy!

www.mascotbooks.com

The Duck Parade of Spokane

For more information, please contact:
Mascot Books
560 Herndon Parkway #120
Herndon, VA 20170
info@mascotbooks.com

Library of Congress Control Number: 2016914549

CPSIA Code: PRT1016A
ISBN-13: 978-1-63177-754-7

Printed in the United States

THE DUCK PARADE OF SPOKANE

Written by
Keri Brubaker Ems

Illustrated by Terry Hinkle

What a lovely May day for a parade! The day of the Lilac Festival Parade in Spokane had finally arrived. Old Man Winter had moved out and made way for spring. The lilacs were in full bloom and people gathered early in the morning to set up chairs for a bird's eye view of the parade route. The high school band tuned up, the floats were in order, and the Boy Scout color guard practiced marching, "Left, left, left, right, left!"

High above the street overlooking Riverside Avenue, the sun shone on Mama Duck's nest. Her twelve baby ducklings quacked with excitement as they got ready for their first swim in the Spokane River.

The parade goers cheered as the car of the grand marshal cruised down Riverside Avenue, signaling the start of the parade. Oblivious to the commotion ten feet below the ledge, Mama Duck paced along the high awning and flapped down to the sidewalk amidst the hustle and bustle of the parade onlookers. Her ducklings, just twenty-four hours old, depended on her and it was time to coax them off the ledge and parade them to the river.

From the sidewalk below, Mama began to call to her ducklings, just as the Boy Scouts color guard passed by. *Whack, whack, whack!*

The ducklings were trained to listen and obey their mama. Ignoring the color guard, they peeked over the edge of the nest to the ground below and realized it was a *long* way down.

Joel, a loan officer who worked in the office on the second floor of the bank, had watched the nest for the last few weeks. He couldn't believe his eyes as he realized that Mama was calling her ducklings

d

   o

     w

       n

to her!

Daisy, the first duckling, stepped to the edge of the nest and peered down at Mama on the street below.

Teetering on the edge, Daisy leaped into the air!

She flipped and flopped, tumbled and plopped onto the sidewalk below, right next to Mama Duck.

Dazed and confused, Daisy lay there, limp and sore.

Joel, watching in horror, rushed to the stairs and leapt three at a time to get to the sidewalk below the nest. He waited like a baseball catcher as the ducklings stepped to the edge of the nest while their mama called them from the street below. Whack, whack, whack!

Dolly bravely stepped to the edge of the nest and gracefully

flipped and

t u m b l e d

flopped,

and plopped

right into...

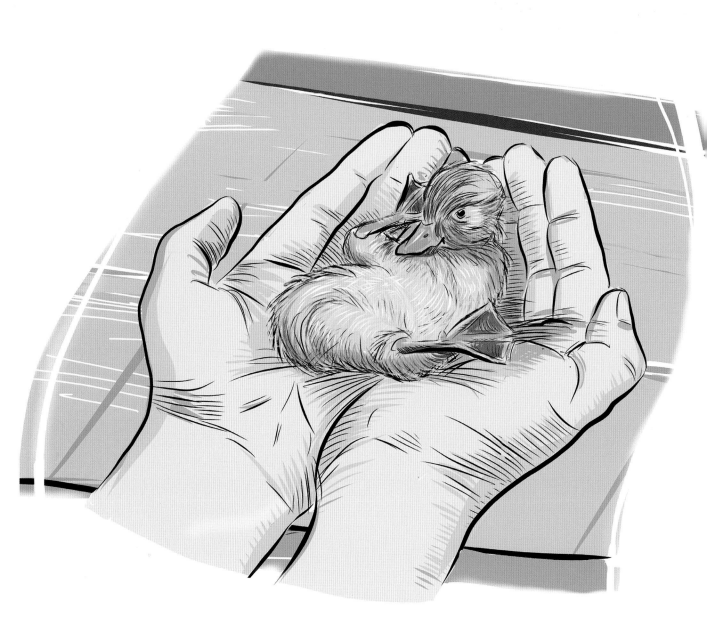

Joel's big hands! He caught Dolly before she hit the sidewalk and set her gently on the ground near her mama.

Next came Dottie. But as she peered over the edge to find Mama, all she saw were Joel's big hands waiting to catch her. Now Dottie was not brave and she stepped away from the edge.

Realizing the dilemma, Joel's friend, Steve, joined him on the ground. Joel stepped out of duckling view while Steve watched the ducklings from a few yards away, warning Joel each time a duckling leaped into the air.

Whack, whack, whack! Mama called from the street.

No ducklings.

Whack, whack, whack! Mama called again.

Over the edge peeked Dottie. Seeing only Mama, Dottie leaped into the air…

flipped,
    flopped,
        tumbled,
            and plopped,

right into the safety of Joel's hands. Quickly setting Dottie down next to Mama, Joel ducked under the roof again to wait.

As floats, fire trucks, and the high school band passed by, none of the ducklings seemed to notice. They only listened for the familiar, **Whack, whack, whack!** of Mama Duck.

Dugger, Dobey, and Duncan teetered on the edge of the nest,
listening for Mama Duck's call.
Whack, whack, whack!

flip,
    flop,
        tumble,
            plop,

flip,
flop,
tumble,
plop,

flip,
flop,
tumble,
plop.

Each landed safely into Joel's hands and was set on its feet near Mama Duck.

By now, the parade goers had two spectacles to watch—the Lilac Festival Parade and the duck diving. As the ducklings on the ground huddled under Mama's protective wing, she called once again. *Whack, whack, whack!*

Up stepped Dexter, Dorrie, and Dewey.

flip,
   flop,
      tumble,
         plop,

flip,
flop,
tumble,
plop,

flip,
flop,
tumble,
plop.

All safe on the ground, thanks to Joel!

Hooray! The ducklings were almost reunited on the ground and ready for their own parade to the river.

Mama called to the last three. Whack, whack, whack!

But Daphne, Della, and little Domino were too frightened to jump.

Now what would Mama Duck do? She couldn't head to the river for a swim without her whole brood.

Parade watchers, now fully aware of the duckling dilemma, couldn't take their eyes off the flurry of activity happening right alongside the Lilac Festival Parade.

Whack, whack, whack! Mama tried again.

The crowd waited. No luck.

Suddenly, a ladder appeared!

"Hooray!" cheered the onlookers.

Joel slowly climbed the ladder, trying not to scare the last three ducklings into jumping with no one to catch them.

Would he be able to rescue Daphne, Della, and little Domino?

Gently, he lifted each duckling out of the nest and set it on the ground to join the others.

The crowd cheered as the last ducklings joined Mama and the others.

Mama Duck quacked, **Whack, whack, whack!** and the ducklings began to follow. Daisy, recovering from her flip, flop, tumble, and plop, shook her tail feathers and staggered along with her brothers and sisters.

The crowd watched as a new parade began. A duck parade!

Mama Duck, followed by Daisy, Dolly, Dottie, Dugger, Dobey, Duncan, Dexter, Dorrie, Dewey, Daphne, Della, and last of all, little Domino, waddled right down Riverside Avenue like a grand marshal, leading her twelve ducklings. Joel and Steve marched right alongside, guiding their new friends on the three-block walk to the Spokane River.

At the river's edge, the ducklings were now expert jumpers.

flip,
flop,
tumble,
plop,

flip,
flop,
tumble,
plop,

flip,
flop,
tumble,
plop.

All the ducklings jumped into the river behind Mama Duck, who was swimming in circles and wagging her tail.

As the sun sparkled on the Spokane River, the ducklings
followed Mama.

Whack, whack, whack! they quacked to thank the townspeople as they swam off together.

DUCK FACTS:

- Ducklings are almost exclusively insect eaters, only turning to a mainly vegetarian diet as they get older.

- A duck doesn't feed her brood, as they are capable of finding their own food as soon as they leave the nest.

- Once all the eggs have hatched, the duck leads the brood away to water. They never return to the nest.

- A typical clutch is from 9 to 13 eggs, but as many as 18 laid by the same duck has been recorded.

- Incubation takes 27 to 28 days, and all the eggs hatch within the same 24-hour period.

- Ducks will lay their eggs in a wide variety of sites, from grassy riverbanks to the tops of tower blocks. The downy young can survive jumps from great heights.

- Though they will pair up in the autumn, the drake only remains with his partner until she starts incubating, and has nothing to do with rearing the ducklings.

- Only the female, or duck, makes the familiar quacking. The drake's call is a much softer and quieter note.

- The mallard's success is due to its adaptability, for it is as much at home on a town pond as it is on a Highland loch.

Source: http://www.rspb.org.uk/community/wildlife/f/13609/t/9479.aspx

ABOUT THE AUTHOR:

Keri has been a teacher for many years. She is an animal lover who always had animals in her classroom, including guinea pigs, mice, hamsters, gerbils, chinchillas, rabbits, snakes, bearded dragons, and even a duck that hatched in her classroom. But that's a tale for another story. Keri lives in Kirkwood, Missouri, a suburb of St. Louis. She loves working with children and writing stories to share with them. You can visit Keri at her website, keriems.com or find her on Facebook at Keri Ems Author.

ABOUT THE ILLUSTRATOR:

Terry has been creating art since he was old enough to hold a crayon. He started his career as a commercial artist, illustrator, and designer but quickly moved to the creative business of advertising and promotion as an art director/creative director. Now Terry enjoys focusing his talents on children's books and his painting. Terry lives in Kirkwood, Missouri with his wife, two daughters, cat, and dog. He and Keri have been friends for many years and plan to do more books together. You can visit Terry on Facebook at HinkleArt.

Creating the illustrations for this book-

After Keri and I talked about her vision of what this book should look like, I started sketching some ideas for her to approve. I usually do my illustrations traditionally, but I wanted to give this modern story a modern look, so I decided to create them digitally.

I started sketching on my new Apple iPad Pro with my Apple Pencil using Adobe Illustrator Draw, one of the new fun drawing apps made for digital touch screens.

Below is the layering process that I went through for one of the baby ducks jumping out of the nest.

After the individual illustrations were approved by Keri, I put each of them through Adobe Photoshop on my Apple MacBook Pro to clean them up and get them ready to send to the publisher.

This was a fun creative process. "QUACK!" -Terry